The Sea At Mughain

A Novella

By Jennifer Sparlin

THE SEA AT MUGHAIN
BY JENNIFER SPARLIN

Cover illustration © 2010 by Marge Simon
Cover design by Atomic Fly Studios

First Printing, February 2010

Sam's Dot Publishing
P.O. Box 782
Cedar Rapids, Iowa, 52406-0782 USA
e-mail: sdpshowcase@yahoo.com

Visit www.samsdotpublishing.com for online science fiction, fantasy, horror, scifaiku, and more. While you are there, visit the Sam's Dot Publishing Purchase Center at http://www.samsdotpublishing.com/purchasecenter.htm for paperbacks, magazines, and chapbooks. **Support the small, independent press...**

For Derek

(no shamrocks)

Where is the hall at the end of the day
And the king feasting?
Where is the fire to warm a guest
At travel's end?
Where is the song that cheered the king
Before the darkness of night falls
The waves crash forever
But the hall is no more.

PROLOGUE

There is a fair green country called Ireland, which lies in the midst of the sea and has birthed many poets and fought many wars. Fifteen hundred years ago, before Ireland was called Ireland, it was divided into many smaller kingdoms, each of which had many poets and many warriors. At that time there were more forests and more magic, and people knew more about some things than we do today, and less about others.

One of the kingdoms in the north of what is now Ireland was called Dal nAraide. The king of Dal nAraide was Tiernan and he ruled from the great hall of Lisnalinchy, a mile from the sea. At the end of each day, the doors of the hall were shut against the night and the mist that rolled up from the sea, and the king and his household ate the daymeal.

One night in particular, however, would be different for the king's sixteen-year old daughter, Mughain.

CHAPTER I
THE HOSTAGE

Mughain nibbled at a chicken leg and stared at the hostage.

He was very interesting to look at. He had medium brown hair and his eyebrows were drawn together in a scowl. In fact, he looked like he only had one eyebrow. He was sitting at a lower table, obviously trying very hard to be polite to the minor lord sitting beside him. He looked like he would rather be anywhere than here.

Mughain looked around. It wasn't such a bad place, she thought. The hall of Lisnalinchy was a large room warmed by several fires in pits that ran down the middle of the floor. On either side of the firepits ran a long table – the low tables. At the end of the hall away from the door was a low dais. On the dais was the high table, where Mughain sat with her family.

The king, Mughain's father, sat in the center of the table. To his right were his three sons, Mughain's half-brothers. To his left sat Mughain's mother, the queen, under a small canopy to protect her from drafts. To her left sat Mughain.

Mughain took a piece of oatcake and nibbled it. For some reason she kept watching the hostage. He was staring down at the table now, ignoring the growing sounds of hilarity around him. The communal cup of ale shared by each table had been filled several times, and everyone was laughing a lot.

Finally, the king finished eating and stood up. "Welcome, friends, to the hall of Dal nAraide!" he said.

Everyone cheered – well, almost everyone. Mughain noticed that the hostage remained seated and wore a tight smile.

"Is there any business this evening?" the king asked. "Do any here seek justice or ask for favor? Speak, and you will be heard."

The hostage rose and walked to stand in front of the high table, facing the king. He was about eighteen, Mughain decided, still watching him with interest. Of medium height, he wore a dull green tunic and brown breeches. His hair fell past his shoulders, and was held back at the sides with two small braids. His eyes were light greenish-brown. He would have been handsome, Mughain decided, if he had two eyebrows.

"I am Brendan, son of Conall, king of Dal Riata," the hostage announced firmly. "I am here as hostage to your goodwill, while you and my father settle the disagreement between you." A low murmur ran through the crowd. "I pledge to stay here eleven days or until you release me." He unsheathed his sword and offered it to the king.

"I accept your pledge, Brendan son of Conall of Dal Riata," said the king calmly. "You may keep your weapon, on your honor, as no man cares to be without means to defend himself. You may come and go as you please during the day, but if you are not in this hall by sunset for the daymeal your life is forfeit."

Brendan bowed his head in agreement. He turned around and went back to his seat at the low table.

Mughain remembered vaguely that there was some disagreement between her father and the king of Dal Riata about cows. Some cows had strayed through a broken fence, and now both kings were arguing about whose cows were whose.

"Are there other matters?" asked the king.

Two men walked into the torchlight from the back of the hall, where they had been waiting for the meal to end. Between them they led a girl about Mughain's age. Her face was dirty and bruised, her dress was torn, and her shift dragged the ground on one side. She was very pretty, and her tangled hair was a color Mughain had never seen before. It was a deep, rich gold that shimmered in the torchlight.

"My lord king," began one of the men ingratiatingly, "I am Eunan son of Eunan. We captured this girl on a raid, and as she is no further use to us, we thought that your household might benefit – for a reasonable price – "

The girl was staring at the floor, as though she was past

9

caring what happened to her.

The king sighed. "What's your name, girl?" he asked.

The girl looked up at him, but did not speak. Her eyes were a bright, forget-me-not blue.

The king frowned at Eunan. "Is she deaf?"

"No – no, my lord," said Eunan. "She just doesn't talk."

"She screams, though," said the other man helpfully. "Her name's Gwyneth, that's what they were yelling when we —"

"The king doesn't have time to hear you babble," Eunan interrupted, sounding a little panicked. The king had leaned forward and put his hands flat on the table, and he was frowning. "If you want --"

"Mughain!" the king shouted, turning his head to look down the table at his daughter. "You're sixteen now, you could use your own handmaid. Do you want her?"

"Yes, father," said Mughain promptly. The golden-haired girl was once again staring at the floor.

Eunan was rubbing his hands together, smiling. "Shall we discuss the matter of —"

"Leave the girl," said the king. "My steward will arrange to pay you. Then get out of my sight."

The two men backed away, bowing. The girl stood alone in the middle of the floor.

The queen turned her head and gestured to the middle-aged maidservant standing behind her chair, who nodded and hurried over to the girl. "Come along, dearie," she said encouragingly. "We'll get you something to eat and something decent to wear."

She put her hand on the girl's arm, but she still stood and stared at the floor.

"It's all right, Brona," said Mughain, rising. "I'll take care of her." She went to the girl and took her arm. "Come with me, please, Gwyneth," Mughain said quietly.

The girl allowed herself to be led. Mughain took her past the high table toward the family apartments. Her mother was glaring at Gwyneth, not at all pleased. She didn't like to have any young, pretty servants around. Usually she sent them to

10

work in the fields.

The buzz of conversation resumed as Mughain took Gwyneth out of the hall. The bard plucked a few notes on the harp. Mughain led the way to her own room, which was curtained off from the rest of the family apartments. A torch burned in a bracket in the one wooden wall, and Mughain's bed and a chest to store her things were the only furnishings. But it was warm and comfortable. The bed had blue and green coverings and there were sheepskin rugs on the floor. A small bronze mirror hung on the wall next to the torch.

"This is my room," said Mughain cheerfully. "You'll be staying in here with me."

Gwyneth said nothing. Brona brought in a basin of water, a linen towel, and a brown wool dress. Another servant followed with a basket of food and some blankets. Gwyneth cringed.

"It's all right, you can leave them," said Mughain quickly. "Thank you."

After the others left, Mughain wet the towel and held it out, trying to wash Gwyneth's face. "It's all right," said Mughain. "No one will hurt you here."

Mughain knew what happened on raids. A boat would suddenly sweep in from the sea and surprise an isolated farm or village. The food and valuables were stolen, the men and old women were killed and the young women and children were taken as slaves. Her father and brothers went on raids. It was the way of things. Her father even had several children by slaves. But no slave girl at Lisnalinchy had bruises, and none were too afraid to speak.

Gwyneth took the cloth and began to wipe her face. She had a large bruise on her left cheek, and another one showed just above the torn neck of her dress. It occurred to Mughain that Gwyneth probably had other bruises on her body, bruises she would not want anyone to see.

"That's right," Mughain said encouragingly. "I forgot something out in the hall, I'll be right back."

She slipped through the curtains and back into the hall.

Eunan and his companion were still bickering with her father's steward, trying to get as many cows as possible for one frightened girl. The bard was singing, accompanying himself on the harp.

"There was a lady with eyes like the sea
From gazing out to the horizon
Before the next wave came to shore she was gone
And she'll never come back to me, to me
And she'll never come back to me."

Mughain crept back to her place at table and picked up her handkerchief. She was trying not to make any noise, but the hostage turned and looked at her.

"There was a lady with eyes like a storm
The wildest that roll in with thunder
And before the next wave crashed to shore she was gone
And I'll search the world over but never,
Never, never will she come back to me."

The firelight flickered on the harp. Mughain broke the connection with the hostage's eyes and slipped back through the curtains, her cheeks burning.

The towel was folded neatly by the basin, the food was gone from the basket, and Gwyneth was rolled up in her blankets, apparently asleep. Mughain undressed quietly and crawled into bed, while the music continued in the hall. Soon the fires would burn low, the tables would be moved aside, and the men would go to sleep on straw pallets on the floor.

Mughain drifted to sleep on the notes of the harp, but angry hazel eyes and frightened blue eyes danced uneasily together in her dreams.

*   *   *

Screaming filled the night, screaming and screaming. Mughain scrambled out of bed as her father burst through the curtains, naked, his sword in his hand, several of his men

12

behind him.

Gwyneth was screaming, thrashing around in her blankets. The king shook his head. "At least we know she's not mute," he said. "Settle her down." He went out through the curtains and the men grumbled their way back out to the hall.

Mughain knelt next to Gwyneth. She was no longer screaming, but she was still thrashing around, gasping for breath. Mughain didn't know what to do. She reached out and patted her maidservant's arm. "It's all right, it's all right," she said, over and over.

Finally Gwyneth lay still and her breathing slowed. Mughain crawled back into bed, but she found it hard to go back to sleep.

*   *   *

Gwyneth was still asleep when Mughain woke up in the morning. She climbed out of bed and chose a dress to wear – green wool, with a thick band of gold knotwork embroidery around the neck and down the center. She pulled on her shift and dress, combed her long, dark hair, and braided it in one long braid down her back to her waist. She secured it with a leather thong that had a small silver disk fastened in the middle. She peered into her bronze mirror, and her eyes, a strange shade of bluish-greenish-gray, stared back out at her.

Gwyneth was stirring. One bruised arm reached out of the blankets.

"Good morning, Gwyneth," said Mughain tentatively.

Gwyneth opened her eyes and sat up. Mughain smiled at her.

Gwyneth had slept in one of Mughain's own shifts. Mughain helped her into the brown wool dress that Brona had left last night, and combed out her glorious gold hair. Gwyneth must be a Saxon, she thought, from the lands to the east. She had heard that Saxons had yellow hair and blue eyes. It occurred to her that her maidservant was supposed to help her dress, not the other way around.

"Let's go get something to eat," she said.

Mughain led Gwyneth through the curtain and into the

13

hall, where morning sunshine dazzled through the open doors and the high windows. The pallets were stacked neatly against the walls, some of the benches had been pulled out, and people were sitting around wherever they felt like it, eating and chatting.

Mughain got some oatcakes, cold beef, cheese, and strawberries from the table at the side of the hall. "Shall we eat outside?" she said to Gwyneth.

People looked at Gwyneth curiously as the walked through the hall. She was even prettier now that she was clean and combed, even in the brown dress that didn't really fit her, and of course everyone had heard her screaming last night. Gwyneth seemed not to notice or care about the looks and whispers.

They went outside. The hall was surrounded by a high wooden wall which was lined with small buildings – stables, kitchens, smithy, all the buildings necessary for all the people of the king's household. They went out the gates and walked around the wall until they were behind the hall itself, facing the sea. There was a place Mughain liked to go, where she could sit and think and look at the faraway ocean.

It was a tiny, rocky hill, with a few small trees and tiny flowers clinging to the soil between the rocks. One flat rock on the top of the hill looked like it used to have carving on it. Another rock, facing the sea, was sort of shaped like a chair. That was where Mughain liked to sit, and watch the land slope slowly down to the sea, and watch the sea rush up to meet it.

However, today someone was already there. Someone was sitting in the rock chair, staring moodily down at the waves. It was the hostage.

Mughain stopped, startled. No one ever came here but her.

The hostage turned around. His eyebrows were still drawn together in one black line, but his face relaxed slightly when he saw Mughain and Gwyneth. He stood up.

"Good morning," he said. "I hope I'm not in your chair, princess."

Mughain was very particular about her chair. "Um – that's

14

all right," she said. They stood and stared at each other. Neither of them seemed to know what to say.

To Mughain's surprise, Gwyneth reached out and took the bundle of food from her and put it on the flat rock. "Would you like something to eat?" Mughain asked the hostage.

Mughain had grabbed plenty of food for three people. As they sat down, she noticed that Brendan's face had relaxed out of its scowl, giving him two eyebrows. Gwyneth sat down to eat with them, and Mughain did not object.

It was a strange conversation, as Mughain and Gwyneth didn't know Brendan, Mughain and Gwyneth hardly knew each other, and Gwyneth didn't speak.

"This is my favorite place – when it isn't raining," said Mughain.

"I hope I'm not intruding," said the hostage. His eyebrows were drawing together again.

"Not at all," said Mughain quickly. "See, I've brought Gwyneth with me."

Gwyneth said nothing and picked at her food.

Mughain broke a large round oatcake in three pieces and shared it around. "I love the ocean," she said. "I like to be where I can see it."

"I hate being inside walls," said Brendan, glancing up at the hall.

Mughain nodded. Gwyneth, who had apparently eaten enough, wandered down the hill and stood in the sparse grass, gazing out to sea. Mughain took the last strawberries and ate them, watching her.

"The princess serves the hostage and the slave," murmured Brendan.

Mughain looked at him, her eyebrows raised.

"I was in hall last night when they brought Gwyneth, remember," Brendan said quietly. "You're very kind to her."

Mughain finished her strawberries. "It could just as easily be me."

Brendan looked surprised. "Surely you are well guarded here. Your father would never let anyone hurt you. He would rescue you, or ransom you if you were captured."

Mughain shook her head. "I'm not a boy. Most of the time I don't think he notices if I'm here or not."

Brendan's eyebrows had drawn together again. "At least your father didn't —" he stopped.

"Didn't what?"

"My father has five sons," muttered Brendan. "He needed to send a hostage to your father, so he sent me."

"It's good that he chose you, then," said Mughain. "He must have known you wouldn't run away and dishonor him."

"I don't think so," said Brendan. "I think he picked me because he thought he could do without me."

They both stared out to sea.

"You look a lot like your mother," Brendan said abruptly.

"Thank you," said Mughain. She was flattered. Her mother was the most beautiful woman she had ever seen. Her skin was white, her hair was black, and her lips were red. Mughain didn't think she looked much like her mother – her hair and eyes were lighter – but it was nice that someone thought she was pretty. Even a hostage with one eyebrow. She glanced at him sideways, but he was still staring off to sea.

Gwyneth stood up and started to walk around aimlessly.

"I don't want her to wander off," said Mughain. She scrambled down the hill to join Gwyneth. When she looked back, the hostage was walking back towards the hall. A gust of wind blew his hair back from his face, and Mughain blinked. His ears were slightly pointed.

CHAPTER II
SUNDAY

The next day was Sunday. Tiernan of Dal nAraide was a Christian king, so he proudly led his entire household to mass every Sunday morning. They all walked to the tiny stone beehive-shaped church where Father Cedric held mass. Only the family and a few others could actually squeeze in the church, so everyone else stood outside while the priest said mass and gave communion. Afterwards he exhorted them all concerning "Forgetting the Old Ways."

"We walked in darkness for many years," Father Cedric said. "Then St. Patrick came and brought us the light, and we have no more need of the old gods and the old customs. As we can now see the light, let us put away that which is evil."

Mughain shuddered on her bench. Many of the old ways were dreadful. If she had lived just a few generations ago, she would have been sacrificed to the old gods when she was a baby. Every woman's first-born child had been sacrificed. Mughain would have died; her oldest half-brother Congal would have died; several of her half-brothers and sisters born to slaves would have died. She could not imagine what life had been like before St. Patrick came.

After mass, the king went to the priest and invited him to the hall for the afternoon and the daymeal. This happened every Sunday. Father Cedric would look at the tiny hut where he lived behind the tiny church, and then at the laughing groups of people who were hurrying back towards the hall. He always accepted the invitation, and came along to spend the day arguing points of theology with the king.

Today the king started the argument as they all walked along the stony path in the sunshine. The ground was flat here, stretching out to either side, covered in thin green grass and small flowers. A few of the king's sheep grazed in the distance.

"Now, you can't say all the old ways were bad," began the

king. "Take marriage, for example. The church says that a king should have only one wife."

The queen's face turned to ice, and she swept on ahead with some of her women. The king did not notice.

"Say you have a king who marries a wife," the king went on. "Say she bears him no children – or only daughters," he added as an afterthought. "A king must have sons, you'll agree."

"Well, yes," said the priest.

"According to the church, what should this king do?" asked the king.

"Well," said the priest reluctantly, "a man may put away a barren wife."

The king shook his head. "I don't think so. Throw her out in the cold to starve? No. The proper solution is to marry a new wife to bear sons, and take care of them both."

This argument continued back and forth throughout the afternoon in the hall. Only necessary daily work, such as tending the animals, cooking, and guarding the hall was ever done on Sundays. Mughain rarely did any work at any time. She didn't like the way Gwyneth's brown dress didn't fit her, so she sent her to lie down in her room and sat down in the hall, where there was light, to take in the side seams and let down the hem of the dress and listen to the argument.

"This was not true in your case," said the priest. "Your first wife bore you three sons, yet you married another wife."

The king was shaking his head and smiling. "No, that was different. My first queen, Tressa, was Queen Nessa's older sister. I married Tressa first, who bore me Congal. Then I married Nessa, because she was Tressa's sister and sisters should not be parted. Then Tressa bore me Domnall and Rory. Nessa has no sons."

No, only me, thought Mughain, viciously poking her iron needle through the brown wool.

Brendan came up and sat next to her. "So your aunt is dead?" he asked quietly.

"Tressa? Yes, she died giving birth to Rory, just after I

was born. I don't remember her." Mughain was absently embroidering blue flowers around the neck of her maidservant's dress.

"And your half-brothers are also your first cousins?" continued Brendan.

"Yes," said Mughain. "Close kinsman to me."

"But not close to you," said Brendan, watching her intently.

No, her half-brothers were not close to her at all. They were interested in war, hunting, war, raiding, war, drinking, and war. They had never had a word to spare for a little sister. Mughain glared at Brendan. "You're very inquisitive," she said.

"You're very pretty," said Brendan.

Mughain stood up, her cheeks flaming. "I have to take this to Gwyneth," she said. She hurried across the hall and through the curtains. She felt Brendan's eyes on her, but did not notice her father watching her with a frown.

The day grew old. The sun dipped to the west, toward the blessed lands of the old stories, and the tables were set up for the daymeal. The priest blessed the food and, as a guest, sat at the high table at the king's right hand. He and the king continued their discussion.

"Say a king has three wives —"

Next to Mughain, Queen Nessa was radiating ice. Everyone in the room but the king could feel it. The priest tried to change the subject several times, carefully not looking at the queen, but it didn't work.

"This is excellent oatcake."

"It is, isn't it? So the king with the three wives —"

It was no use. The king would never understand that Nessa had hated her sister, and hated any woman the king even looked at. Mughain was grateful that he had shown no interest in Gwyneth, who was silently standing behind her chair.

The feast was over when the king was done eating. "I should be getting back home," said Father Cedric.

"Nonsense," said the king. "It's already dark. What kind

19

of a host would I be, letting a guest go home in the dark? You'll sleep here in this hall, under my roof with my men."

They had this discussion every Sunday as well, and the king always had his way in the end. "A Sunday story for our priest!" he said to the hall.

The bard stood up and plucked his harp. "The Story of St. Patrick," he said. The hall cheered.

Mughain turned to Gwyneth. "Go and eat with the others, and when you're finished, you may come back and listen to the stories or go to bed as you like," she said.

Brona took Gwyneth's arm. "Come along, dearie," she said. Gwyneth followed her listlessly.

Mughain hoped Brona would keep an eye on Gwyneth. She didn't want her wandering off in the dark alone.

The bard was chanting the story of St. Patrick, accompanying himself on the harp:

"There was a lad whom the angels sent
To show us the way to the kingdom of heaven
He conquered us with peace and joy
He took us to the throne of God —"

Mughain knew the story of St. Patrick, of course. He was a Breton, from the lands to the east, who had been captured as a slave like Gwyneth. He escaped, but then had a vision that he was to return to the land and people of his captivity and show them the way of salvation. He obeyed his vision, and it was due to St. Patrick that Christianity had come to the kingdoms.

Mughain peered toward the front of the hall, trying to see out into the courtyard.

"A friend was he, a brother was he,
A father was he, a priest was he —"

Mughain was worried about Gwyneth. She stood up and walked past the low tables to the doors of the hall, and out into

20

the courtyard.

Several small fires were lit around the courtyard, and the servants had congregated around them to eat. Mughain spotted Gwyneth, sitting by Brona and quietly eating.

"You're going to have to start trusting her eventually."

Brendan had followed her out into the night. Mughain turned and looked up at him.

"I do trust her," she said indignantly. "I don't think she'll run away on purpose. I just don't want anything to happen to her."

Brendan's face was shadowed and mysterious. Mughain felt her indignation leaving her, to be replaced by a strange feeling in her stomach, as though she had swallowed several butterflies.

"Come and sit down," said Brendan.

They sat on a bench where a thin line of firelight glowed through a crack in the wall. Mughain made sure she could see Gwyneth. Brendan smiled, but changed the subject.

"Will they care that you're out here?" he asked.

Mughain blinked. "I doubt they'll notice," she said. "But it's all right – they wouldn't care. People can come and go as they please between the courtyard and the hall. If people want to talk, they usually come out here. Most people want to hear the stories. Except the servants, of course – they want to eat."

"Don't you like the stories?"

"Don't you?"

Brendan grinned. "I like you better."

Again, Mughain could feel her face burning. She hoped it was too dark for Brendan to see. Of course, she could see him grinning.

"Um – I like the stories," she said. "Father has a good bard."

"I thought about being a bard," said Brendan bitterly, "but my father didn't approve. He said a king needs all his sons with him." Mughain couldn't see his eyebrows, but she was sure that they had drawn together. Out of the corner of her eye, she tried to look at his ears, to see if they were really

21

pointed.

"Would you like to ride with me tomorrow?" he said abruptly. "You and Gwyneth?"

"Ride?" said Mughain blankly.

"We could go to the beach, anywhere. You said you like the sea."

Mughain smiled.

"Then you'll go?"

Brona was bringing Gwyneth to the door of the hall, but stopped when she saw Mughain. "Here she is, my lady," she said. "I think she wanted to come inside to you."

"Thank you, Brona," said Mughain. Gwyneth sat down on the ground by the bench with her arms around her legs and her chin on her knees.

"I'd best see if your lady mother is wanting anything," said Brona, and went into the hall.

"My lady mother," said Mughain, "would like my lord father to stop talking to the priest about *wives*."

"I noticed that," said Brendan.

"What do you think?" said Mughain. "How many wives should a man have?"

"Is that a trick question?"

"Maybe."

"A man or a king?"

"A man."

"A man, one," said Brendan. "A prince – one." Mughain felt herself blushing again. "A king – it depends."

"Depends on what?"

"How many questions his wives ask."

Gwyneth reached out and punched Brendan lightly on the leg. It was the first time she had made any response to anything that had been said around her.

"Good for you, Gwyneth," said Brendan, wincing slightly and rubbing his leg. "Well, what will it be, princess? Will you ride with me tomorrow, you and your faithful bodyguard here, after we break our fast?"

Brona appeared at the door. "My lady, your lady mother

22

would like you to come inside now," she said.

Mughain's eyes widened in surprise. "All right, Brona." She started to stand up, but Brendan caught at her sleeve.

"Come with me tomorrow," he said quietly, staring into her eyes.

The fluttery feeling in Mugain's stomach was back. She nodded slightly, then followed Brona back into the hall, with Gwyneth trailing behind her. Instead of coming with them, Brendan headed off toward the stables.

The hall seemed very bright after the courtyard, and the bard was singing. Mughain slipped into her chair at the high table. "What is it, Mother?"

The queen turned her head slowly and looked at Mughain. As usual, she had very little expression on her beautiful face. "It is damp," she said finally. "You are better off indoors."

"Damp?" Mughain repeated blankly. But the queen had already turned her beautiful face back to the bard.

CHAPTER III
A RIDE TO THE SEA

Mughain woke with her stomach fluttering. For a moment she couldn't remember why. Brendan's face, dimly lit in the firelight in the courtyard, had haunted her dreams.

She chose her blue wool dress to wear. It had red flowers and green leaves embroidered in a band around the neck and at the ends of the sleeves. Gwyneth combed and braided her hair very nicely for her. Then Mughain combed and braided Gwyneth's.

They went out into the hall and got some food, but Mughain didn't really feel like eating. The butterflies were flying around worse than ever. She didn't see Brendan in the hall. She made herself eat some cheese and oatcake, and then collected some more food to take with them on their ride.

The king and the priest were sitting together on a bench, eating and continuing their discussion of the night before. "What you need," said the king, "is a wife of your own."

The priest looked rather panicked, and appeared to choke on his oatcake.

"I know just the girl for you," continued the king. "My daughter, Ita. You've seen her at church."

Mughain hardly knew her half-sister Ita. She was the daughter of the king and a servant. They lived out in one of the little cottages that dotted the king's pastures, and helped look after the sheep. The queen had made sure that neither Ita or her mother were ever anywhere near her.

When they went outside, Brendan was waiting for them by the stables, looking very cheerful and holding the bridle of his light-brown horse. The horse was shaking his head and pawing at the ground, eager to be off.

"Easy, Fergus," said Brendan. "Good morning, princess."

Mughain blushed, which made her angry. "Good morning," she said. "Please bring me two horses," she added to a groom.

Brendan looked surprised. "You don't have your own horse?"

Mughain shrugged. "It doesn't really matter." The groom was bringing out two mares, a roan and a white. Mughain chose the roan and turned to ask the groom to help Gwyneth up, but she was already vaulting easily into the white's saddle.

Mughain raised her eyebrows, but said nothing. Apparently Gwyneth was used to riding horses.

Brendan led the way through the courtyard and out the gate. They rode around the wall until they could see the sea shimmering blue below them.

Brendan drew a deep breath. "This is more like it," he said.

They rode past the little hill with Mughain's rock chair and down the rocky slope to the sea. The ground was too rough to ride very fast. The rocks were broken with low bushes covered with pink flowers, which Mughain and Gwyneth's horses kept trying to eat. Brendan's horse Fergus seemed only interested in trying to run.

"He doesn't like – being – shut up —" Brendan said breathlessly, trying to keep Fergus under control.

Like horse, like owner, thought Mughain.

Before long they were close to the beach. To their right was a natural harbor where the king kept his ship and other boats, and a few of his men to keep watch. Congal was building a ship, too. Its skeleton was propped up on the beach like some enormous animal. Mughain stared gloomily at the harbor. Her other brothers would have their own ships, too, in a few years, but Mughain never would.

"I only got to go out on Father's ship once," she said. "He really only uses it for raids or wars."

"I'll take you out on a boat someday," Brendan promised.

Mughain turned to smile at him, and she saw that his ears were indeed slightly pointed. The wind changed, blowing in directly from the sea. It brought with it the stinging salt smell of the sea and the keening cries of the gulls.

To their left, away from the harbor, was a smooth stretch of beach that swept down to meet the waves. In the distance a large rock formation jutted up out of the sand.

"Race you to that rock!" Brendan yelled suddenly.

The three horses thundered down the beach and ran right along the edge of the sea and the sand. Mughain was laughing. She had never felt so free.

Gwyneth's white horse pulled ahead of the others and streaked toward the rock. Mughain slowed down to watch her. She had never seen anybody ride that fast. Gwyneth was leaning low over her horse, her legs were tucked up under her skirts, and her golden hair had come unbraided and streamed behind her. She looked like a part of the horse. She looked, Mughain realized, like one of the strange half-human, half-animal creatures that peopled the old stories.

Brendan did not slow down, but Gwyneth beat him easily. Close to the rock, she wheeled her horse around, smiling with delight. Truly she was beautiful. The white mare pranced around proudly.

Mughain nudged her horse to a trot and caught up with the others by the rock. Gwyneth's radiance was starting to fade; she was remembering where and who she now was. Brendan swung down off his horse. "Gwyneth wins," he said simply.

No, Mughain thought, looking closely at Gwyneth's face, Gwyneth doesn't win anything at all.

They led their horses around the big rock, and found that it was one arm of a hollow semicircle, like a roofless cave that opened up to the sea. There was a few feet of sand between the edge of the rock and the surf, but at a higher tide, the sea would rise well past the rocks and a person caught in the semicircle would be trapped.

"Let's not stay here long," said Brendan.

It was a calm, pleasant place. The sun warmed the rocks and the sand, and the sea foamed and rippled invitingly at the mouth of the semicircle. There was nowhere to tie the horses, but there was nowhere they could really go. Gwyneth held up her skirts and splashed around in the shallows like a child.

"I never knew this place was here," said Mughain. She sat down in the sand and leaned back on her hands. It was fun to have sand on her toes.

Brendan was looking around with interest. "You can't see it from your father's hall, the edge of the forest starts up there and blocks this whole part of the beach." He prowled around the sheer rock walls. "I don't know if this cave is completely natural," he said. "This stone looks like it's been worked, or carved." He ran his hand along the wall.

"My rock chair is like that," said Mughain.

Brendan padded through the sand and lay down next to Mughain, propped up on one elbow. Mughain gazed out to sea.

"Your eyes have turned the color of the sea," Brendan said softly. "You look at it too much."

Mughain turned her strange bluish-greenish-gray eyes on him. "They've always been like this," she said. "When I was born, my father asked my mother where she'd found a baby mermaid. Then when I was a few years older, he carried me around on his shoulders. He called me his little mermaid, then, too." She turned her eyes back out to sea. "He liked me better then."

Brendan was silent for a little while. "They really don't pay enough attention to you," he burst out. "Nobody ever talks to you or looks after you —"

"I don't need looking after!" said Mughain indignantly.

" – it's like you're alone all the time."

"Is your family any different?" Mughain said bitterly. "Does your father confide in your sisters, or treat them the same as you and your brothers?"

"No," said Brendan, "but my sisters have their own horses."

Mughain stared down at the sand.

"You're a princess," he said, "whether they treat you like one or not."

She looked up at him.

Gwyneth padded up toward them, looking anxious. Mughain saw that the water was closer to the rocks and stood up. "We should go," she said. She was glad for the interruption, because for a moment she was afraid she was either going to cry or fall into Brendan's eyes.

There was now only a foot of sand between the sea and the rocks. They got the horses out without any problem, but Mughain got the hem of her dress wet.

Brendan grinned. "You could take it off and let it dry," he suggested.

"Hit him again, Gwyneth," said Mughain. Brendan ran up the beach, urging Fergus along by the reins. He came back before long, though.

They rode around the rock to see what was on the other side. It was impossible to get down to the beach that way. The rock made a barrier that continued back into the beginnings of the forest. "We'd have to follow it all the way around through the trees," said Brendan.

They followed it for a while, but the trees grew thicker and it became difficult to ride. Mughain didn't like the woods. She felt closed in, and always as though unseen eyes were watching her. She looked around nervously.

"What's wrong?" Brendan asked.

"Nothing." Anything could be hiding in the gloom, behind those still, silent, menacing trees. How could you ever know what was there in the shadows?

Soon they hit a path that cut through the trees. "I know where we are," said Brendan. "This is the road I took to come here – to your father's hall, I mean. That's the way home." He meant his home. He pointed down the path, lined with trees until it was swallowed by the distance.

They could have simply taken the road the other way, back to the hall, but they decided to go back to the beach instead. Mughain was glad. She walked her horse as fast as she dared and breathed easier as the trees thinned. Finally the roan stepped out into the sunlight and she sighed with relief, and waited for the others.

Brendan looked at her curiously as he and Gwyneth emerged from the trees.

"I don't like the woods," said Mughain haughtily.

Brendan looked puzzled, but did not comment.

They rode part of the way back along the beach, and then tied their horses to a low, scrubby tree and ate the food they had brought.

"What's your father's hall like? It's called Dunseverick, isn't it?" asked Mughain. She was spreading her skirt out around her feet to dry. The damp wool was cold against her legs. She wished she *could* just take it off until it dried.

Brendan looked pleased. For a minute Mughain thought he knew what she was thinking, and blushed. Then she realized he was pleased because she knew the name of his home.

"Yes," said Brendan. "It's called Dunseverick. You'd like it. The hall is built on a promontory, so it's surrounded on three sides by the sea."

Mughain's eyes grew wide.

"Good for mermaids, but not for dryads," Brendan remarked.

Mughain looked at him sideways. A dryad was a wood nymph, the female spirit of a tree. "You said you have sisters?" she inquired loftily.

"Two," said Brendan, stretching his legs out in the sand. "Well, really only one. Catlin is my sister-in-law, Deirdre is my sister. You'd like her. She's fifteen. I forget that Cat isn't really my sister, too. She's married to my oldest brother."

Mughain would have liked to have a sister – one who was not shunted off to the sheep farms or the kitchen. She watched Gwyneth wandering around down by the water.

Idly, Brendan was tracing a circle in the sand – the symbol for eternity.

"We should be going back soon," said Mughain. "You have to be back for the daymeal."

Brendan's eyebrows drew together. "I suppose so," he said.

"I – this has been a very nice day," said Mughain.

Brendan looked at her. He put out his hand and touched her cheek, and then stood up and went to untie Fergus. Mughain followed, struggling with the butterflies that danced wildly in her stomach. They left the circle of eternity Brendan had scratched in the sand to the mercy of the incoming tide.

*   *   *

They rode back slowly, not speaking. The light slanted golden from the west, and in the distance the cows and sheep were being brought in for the night, mooing and baaing respectively. They rode into the gates well before sunset and gave their horses to the grooms. Then they all went into the hall together.

The king was pacing back and forth, while all around him the men were trying to stay out of his way while they set up the tables and benches for the daymeal. He caught sight of Mughain and strode toward her. *"Where have you been!"*

Mughain blinked up at him. "I went for a ride."

"A *ride!* A *ride?"* The king was obviously trying to find something wrong with that.

"I was with her, my lord," said Brendan stiffly. "I would not have allowed her to come to harm."

"You," said the king contemptuously.

"I took Gwyneth, too," said Mughain.

The king thought about that, growling to himself.

Mughain was angry and confused. No one had ever taken the least notice of where she was or what she did during the day before. "I don't understand, Father. What did I do wrong? You've always trusted me, I've always done what I saw fit. Why is today different?"

The king looked at Brendan, still standing stiffly a little behind Mughain. "Humph," he said, and strode off.

Gwyneth was white and shaking, and Mughain forgot her own annoyance. "Oh, it's all right, Gwyneth, he's not going to hurt you, no one is going to hurt you." She led her over to the side of the hall, away from the men who were setting up the tables. She looked over her shoulder for Brendan, but he was stomping out the door on his way back out to the stables. Mughain hoped he was just going to take care of his horse. She wondered what had made her father suddenly realize she was alive.

30

CHAPTER IV
STORM

That night a storm blew in off the sea. The wind started moaning around the hall as they were finishing the daymeal, and the torches flickered as gusts forced themselves through cracks in the walls. Mughain lay in bed listening to the pounding of the surf in the distance. She wished she was down on the beach, walking in the storm. Then the rain came in a gust of wind and she dropped off to sleep.

In the morning the rain still pounded on the roof of the hall. Mughain pulled on her gray wool dress with silver knotwork embroidery. Gwyneth combed her dark hair for her and braided it in two long braids, tied together in the back with a leather thong. Mughain sat shivering while Gwyneth braided her own hair. She looked in the chest at the foot of the bed and found her light summer cloak, which was made of thin red wool, and swung it around her shoulders. That was better. She would have to find something for Gwyneth. She rummaged around some more and found an old blue cloak, which was too short and frayed at the hem. It was better than nothing. She draped it around Gwyneth's shoulders and they went out into the hall.

People were breaking their fast huddled around the three firepits. A large cauldron of porridge steamed on the fire nearest the family apartments, farthest from the door. Gwyneth fetched Mughain's porridge and then went to get her own.

Brendan was sitting on a bench by himself, glumly stirring his porridge. Mughain went to him and sat down.

"My lady of the storms," he said by way of greeting, glancing at her gray dress and red cloak, and then back at his porridge.

"When the sea is gray
And the dawn is red

Turn your back on the storm
And go back to bed."

It was something the sailors said. Everyone knew that a red sky at dawn meant a storm.

"Don't you like porridge?" Mughain asked.

"I don't like rain."

Gwyneth brought her porridge and sat down on the floor next to Mughain.

"I love porridge," said Mughain.

"Mermaids don't eat porridge," said Brendan absently.

"You never know, they might have some sort of seaweed porridge," said Mughain.

"How would they cook it?"

Mughain considered this while she finished her porridge. She stood up to get more. Gwyneth reached for her bowl, but Brendan took it first. "I'll get it," he said.

He was frowning when he came back. "The men are saying that the sea is angry," he muttered.

The sea did sound angry. Mughain ate her second bowl of porridge and listened to the wind. The storm seemed to be getting worse. There was a sudden, brilliant flash of lightning and a loud clap of thunder. Gwyneth screamed and huddled close to Mughain's leg.

"It's all right," Mughain said soothingly, stroking Gwyneth's hair.

The wind howled. Every clap of thunder made Gwyneth shake and whimper. Mughain just kept stroking her hair.

"We get storms like this at home," said Brendan. "The hall is much more exposed, out on the cliff."

Mughain thought it sounded wonderful.

The work of the day had to be done, rain or no rain. Men and maids splashed out into the courtyard, laughing and grumbling, to do what had to be done. Some of the children stayed playing in the corner of the hall, the queen and her women sat embroidering, and the king and his sons stood by the door of the hall, talking and looking out into the rain.

But not much could be done in the storm. Slowly the hall filled again with people doing whatever odd jobs that could be done indoors: mending harnesses and clothing, feeding the fires, talking. Everyone was a little restless. Gwyneth was asleep with her head on Mughain's knee; Mughain was falling into a doze, lured by the rain on the roof. Brendan was frowning at the wall.

Some of the maids set up a loom nearby and began to weave. "Click, clack, click clack, click, clack," went the loom.

"That's ridiculous," said Brendan.

Mughain opened her eyes; apparently she had gone to sleep. The hall was a little darker, the torches had been lit, and the storm still raged. Gwyneth was awake, sitting up against the bench. Brendan was holding a knife in one hand and a stick of wood in the other, which he was apparently carving into something. His eyebrows formed one straight line.

"What?" yawned Mughain.

"Listen," he said quietly.

"Click, clack, click, clack," went the loom. Derval, one of the maids, was talking to the others.

"It's true, the sea is angry," she was saying. She nodded significantly toward the back of the hall, in the direction of the raging sea. "In the old days, there were women as could tell the sea when to be angry, and when to be calm."

Fidelma, one of the other maids, made the sign of the cross. "That's bad luck, to speak of such things," she said. "Take it back."

Click, clack, clickety-clack.

Derval sniffed. "I'll say what I like," she said. "Some things were better in the old days. Sure and the women had a better time of it. No priests telling us what to do, and such."

Mughain wondered if Derval would have thought herself better off if she had lived in the old days and had to sacrifice her firstborn child.

"I like the priest," said Devnet, the third maid.

Derval shook her head. "You like any fine-looking man," she said.

"I do not," began Devnet, but Derval interrupted her. "The old ways are best," she said importantly.

"She has no idea what she's talking about," said Brendan. He was glowering down at the piece of wood he was holding. It looked vaguely like a fish.

Mughain wondered how long she had been asleep. The queen came over to the maids, looked at their weaving, and pointed out something she wanted done differently. "Make the border a little wider, Derval," she said. "This is for a wall hanging, so we'll want to be able to see the pattern across the room."

"Yes, my lady."

The queen glided over to stand in front of Mughain. She looked at Gwyneth. "You must get this child a better cloak."

"Yes, mother," said Mughain. She was very puzzled. Her mother very rarely spoke to her, and never about cloaks.

The queen's eyes traveled to Brendan. Then she turned and went back to sit with her women.

"That was strange," said Mughain.

"I thought it was nice," said Brendan. He was alternately frowning at his wood carving and the three maids, who were folding up the loom and putting it against the wall out of the way.

It was colder. Mughain huddled in her cloak. The kitchen servants brought the big cauldrons back in the hall, but instead of porridge they were filled with clams, seaweed, and leeks. They put one cauldron over each firepit, and soon the smell of stew filled the hall. Mughain's stomach rumbled.

The men set up the tables and benches for the daymeal. The servants brought in bread and ale from the kitchens, trying and failing to keep the bread dry. At least the stew would be hot and thick, since it had been cooked in the hall. Brendan put his carving away and went to help with the benches, and Mughain went to take her place beside the queen at the high table.

She was stiff and sore from napping all day, and still felt half asleep. It was time for sunset, but no red glow showed through the cracks in the shutters that covered the high windows. The gray day was deepening into a black and howling night.

The household took their places around the tables, and the king reached for a piece of bread. The daymeal was about to begin. But before the king could eat, his steward stepped forward.

"My lord," he said, "there is one outside who would fast the king."

The king stared at him. *"Tonight?"*

"Yes, my lord. It is Breasal son of Corval. He would like an answer from the king regarding his markers."

The king swore. Breasal and his neighbor had been disputing their property line for a year. The heavy stone markers had been moved back and forth several times, usually in the dead of night, by young relatives of Breasal and his neighbor. It was something of a joke in the neighborhood. But it was no joke for old Breasal to be out in the rain on a night like this one. He must desperately want a judgment on where the property line would be drawn.

Any man could approach a king. Any man could ask favor. But the king, of course, never had to make a decision – unless he was fasted. Fasting meant that Breasal would wait outside the king's door, eating nothing, until he got an answer about his markers. There was no time limit, of course, for the king to make his decision – but the king could not eat either until he gave one.

The king dropped his piece of bread and wiped his fingers on his tunic. "Bring him in," he said sharply. "Breasal!"

Breasal hobbled into the hall, supported by one of his nephews. "The king is gracious to hear me," he whined.

"The king is hungry," said the king.

"My lord," replied old Breasal. "Some things are more important to an old man than food."

"Such as *property markers?*"

"It's a wise king you are, my lord." Breasal's nephew, who undoubtedly had moved the property markers at least once himself, nodded in agreement.

The king sighed. "The priest has been telling us about a wise king named Solomon," he said. "I will pass judgment as Solomon did. The property in dispute will be divided down the center. Half will be yours and half will be your neighbor's. This is my judgment; I have answered. Now sit and eat. You are welcome to my hall."

Old Breasal looked disappointed, but he bowed his head and shuffled off after the steward to a place at one of the lower tables. His nephew followed.

"Property stones," remarked the king to no one in particular, "are of course as binding as law, a witness between neighbors."

Breasal's nephew looked slightly guilty. It was almost certain that as soon as old Breasal got bored, the markers would be moved again.

The king glared around the hall. "Is there anything else?" he demanded.

No one answered, so the king reached, once again, for his piece of bread. The daymeal had begun. He put the flat piece of bread on the table, poured some clam stew on top, and began eating. Rory's dog snuffed hopefully at his feet in case he didn't want his gravy-soaked bread.

Mughain glanced down the tables at Brendan. He was talking to Breasal's nephew, who looked very interested in whatever he was saying. Behind her, Mughain heard Gwyneth give a small sigh. She broke off a piece of bread and passed it behind her, careful not to let her mother see. She felt Gwyneth's fingers take the bread, equally carefully. The rain kept pounding on the roof.

When the king had eaten and drunk enough, it was time for songs and stories. Most of the servants, including Gwyneth, had huddled at the front of the hall to eat the leftovers of the daymeal. The king looked around at the quiet and shivering hall.

"This won't do!" he said. "Let's be friendly tonight. Move the tables back and put the benches around the fires.

We'll have cold backs but warm hearts!"

The men obeyed, moving the benches into one long oval that circled the three firepits. The king and his family still sat near one end, but somehow the feeling of upper and lower tables had been lost. Many of the servants were in the circle, finishing their meal, and somehow Brendan ended up sitting next to Mughain.

"Oh, is that you?" he asked, pretending to be surprised.

"Now," said the king, "let's have a song to warm us."

They sang one song after another, the kind they could clap their hands and stomp their feet to, the kind that would drive away the cold and the damp and the uneasy thoughts of an angry sea. Mughain glimpsed Derval, the maid who liked the old ways, lustily singing at the other end of the circle.

Then someone started dancing, weaving a pattern around the firepits, and someone else joined, and Brendan grabbed Mughain's hand and whirled her into the dance. Everyone who wasn't dancing was cheering and keeping time with hands and feet. Out of the corner of her eye Mughain saw the king dancing with a maid and the queen glaring, Gwyneth dancing with Breasal's nephew, Gwyneth golden-haired laughing, the firelight spinning, but what she saw most was Brendan, Brendan's face close to hers, Brendan's two eyebrows and Brendan's strange hazel eyes and smiling lips, and she had a strange feeling in her stomach and a stranger feeling that she and Brendan had always been dancing beside the fire . . .

Laughing, gasping, people started to sit down, holding their sides and no longer cold at all. The king was laughing harder than anyone. "A song!" he called. "A restful song!"

The bard shook his head; he was too out of breath from dancing to speak. The king roared with laughter. So did everyone else. "A song!" he said. "Anyone who can carry a tune!"

Brendan stood up. "I have a song."

The king stiffened slightly and some of the laughter left his face, but he nodded, so Brendan crossed the circle to where the bard sat with his harp. "May I?" asked Brendan. The bard still could not speak, but he nodded and moved aside.

"This is a song," Brendan said, "about the future of my father's kingdom."

There were nods and murmurs of approval among the fading laughter. Songs about the future usually involved one of many noble descendants of a living king. This descendant would recall with pride and great detail the brave exploits of his grandsire, who after an amazingly long life set sail west toward the blessed lands. In recent years the blessed lands had somehow got mixed up with St. Patrick's heaven, but that only added more glory to the songs and the revered ancestor.

Brendan plucked a few notes on the harp. They had a strange, lonely sound, like drops from a waterfall in a forest never seen by mortal eyes. Then Brendan started to sing. His voice was clear and pure, a little higher than his speaking voice.

"Now are the sounds of battle stilled
And a still green path
Leads to the broken tower
Overlooking the sea.
Look to the north, Dunseverick,
Ancient seat of kings.

Where is the hall at the end of the day
And the king feasting?
Where is the fire to warm a guest
At travel's end?
Where is the song that cheered the king
Before the darkness of night falls
The waves crash forever
But the hall is no more.

Before the broken tower
The kings of Dal Riata
Looked out to sea
And plotted conquest.

But now
A smooth, green, secret turf
Hides the place of the hall
The laughter of kings is in the waves
The song of the hall is in the wind
Caressing the broken tower."

The hall had gone silent. Brendan looked up from the harp to see stares of disapproval.

"A fine voice, lad," said the bard hastily. "I'll take the next one." He started strumming the harp and singing a more conventional song as Brendan stumbled back across the circle to Mughain.

But it was too late. The cold and the damp were back, the storm raged outside and the sea beat against the shore, the spell that had been broken by singing and dancing was back. Men and maids whispered and muttered and glanced, and the king sat with his arms folded, staring straight ahead.

Brendan's eyebrows were drawn together. "They didn't like it," he muttered.

"It wasn't what they were expecting," said Mughain.

Brendan glared. "You didn't like it either."

"It made me feel – strange," Mughain said. It had not been a good choice, she thought, for a night such as this one. "I don't like thinking – of being forgotten, of nobody ever knowing – ever remembering us – me —"

Mughain blushed, but Brendan was too preoccupied to notice that she had included the two of them, together, in what she wanted future generations to remember. "It's like the stone circles," he argued, "and the standing stones, and the old portal tombs. No one knows who built those, no one remembers them."

Mughain shifted uncomfortably. She didn't like the stone circles even in the daylight. Here and there they stuck out of the green turf like broken gray teeth. Some were still carved with strange symbols. There was an eerie feeling about them, like something was there that could not be seen. In the old days the Druids, the priests, had used them for celebrations, but the Druids had not built them. No, she did not want to think about them at night, during a storm. "No one wants to be forgotten," she said.

Brendan turned his strange hazel eyes on her. His eyebrows had relented somewhat, and the firelight caught the shadow of one pointed ear. "Will you forget me?" he said softly. "After I go home, I mean."

The king stood abruptly. "Sleep well," he barked, and strode toward the family apartments. It was time to go to bed. The queen hurried after the king; her women followed; the men started pushing the benches against the wall and unstacking the straw pallets on which they slept. Thunder crashed; lightning illuminated every crack in the walls.

"I will never forget you," said Mughain.

Brendan's hand reached out to Mughain's, his lips opened to speak, but one of her father's men good-naturedly punched him in the shoulder. "Help me with this bench, princeling," he said.

Brendan turned to help with the bench, with a last look over his shoulder at Mughain. Mughain looked around for Gwyneth, found her wandering toward her, and led her off to her room. She glanced back, but Brendan and her father's men were throwing pallets on the floor at a safe distance from the fires.

Stone circles and forgotten towers, firelight and dancing with Brendan's arm around her waist and the laughter of her mute handmaiden in her ears. Mughain was not sure she would be able to sleep, but the storm lulled her away.

CHAPTER V
AT THE BEACH

The next day dawned smiling, acting as though it had never rained before and never intended to do so again. The sea was a mild and deceptive blue-green with tiny white waves; a warm gentle breeze stirred the seagrass. But the king and his sons broke their fast quickly, sitting in a huddle and frowning. They had been down to the harbor at dawn. The storm had driven the king's ship onto the beach and completely through the skeleton of Congal's half-completed one. The king's ship could be repaired, but Congal's could not. They would have to start over and build a new one.

"We should have beached the ships," said Congal.

The king shook his head. "How could we have known? I've never seen a storm like this, this time of year."

Outside the men were busy making minor repairs to the hall and tightening the thatch. Some of the timbers on the seaward side were loose, and a few had blown away. One piece of wood stuck straight up in the middle of the thatched roof of the smithy.

Brendan came in from the direction of the stable and sat down next to Mughain on the bench where she and Gwyneth were eating. "Come for a walk with me," he said.

"You don't want to ride?" said Mughain.

Brendan shook his head. "Fergus is still spooked from the storm; I think he'd throw me. Besides, I want to talk to you."

"Yes, my lord."

Brendan glared at her, his eyebrows pulled together. "Fine. Will you please walk with me, that I may share with you my thoughts upon diverse matters?"

"Yes, my lord."

Brendan stomped out of the hall. Mughain and Gwyneth grinned at each other and finished their breakfast.

Brendan was waiting for them in the courtyard. The sun was warm, but his gray cloak swung from his shoulders. They walked out of the gate and around the wall and the men repairing it, past Mughain's rock chair and down the rocky slope toward the smiling sea.

"Do you want to see the ships?" said Mughain.

Brendan just nodded; he was still out of sorts. The harbor was full of men, standing around the splintered wreck of Congal's unfinished ship. It made Mughain sad to see it.

"It will never sail," she said softly. The gentle breeze stirred, lifting her hair away from her neck.

Brendan looked at her. His eyebrows were back to two. "Let's walk along the beach."

Driftwood littered the beach from the storm. A few of the men and maids were out gathering it; driftwood was good for fuel, and made interesting carvings or furniture. Sometimes it had strange curves and patterns that had been sculpted by the sea. The king's bed was made of driftwood, appropriate for a sea king.

The farther from the harbor they walked, the more alone they were. A few gulls circled and cried. Mughain took off her shoes and walked along the edge of the gentle surf, but there were a lot of broken shells from the storm.

"Ouch."

Gwyneth held out Mughain's shoes, but Brendan gallantly waded in and picked her up. Mughain squealed. "You're going to get your dress wet again," he said. He was holding her close to him.

Then the blue sky and the blue sea whirled around and Mughain had to shut her eyes to keep from getting dizzy, because Brendan was kissing her. All she knew was that her arms were around Brendan's neck and her fingers were caught in his hair, and nothing existed in the world except the sea and the sky and Brendan, and the gulls still crying in the distance.

"Your feet are getting wet," she said in his ear.

"Yes," he said. He carried her a few steps up on the beach and put her down.

Abruptly Mughain remembered Gwyneth. She turned around to find her, but Gwyneth was very intently studying the sky.

"Gwyneth," Brendan said politely, "do you mind if I talk to Mughain alone for a few minutes?"

Gwyneth gave Brendan a very knowing smile and sat down in the sand. Brendan grabbed Mughain's hand and they ran along the beach until they felt like they were alone. Mughain's heart was pounding, but not from running. She wanted to laugh and cry and fly, all at once. But she made sure she could still keep an eye on Gwyneth.

Brendan pulled Mughain down to sit beside him in the sand. "I'm going to ask your father for you," he said.

"What if I say no?"

Brendan kissed her again.

"Come home with me," he said. "Be my princess."

The sun shone on his hair, turning it deep gold. He was smiling, and his ears were pointed, and his eyes glowed next to the sea.

"Yes," said Mughain . . .

The tide seemed to be higher than it should. Mughain frowned at it. Surely Brendan had just started kissing her a few minutes ago. They had talked about things too, she realized; how happy his parents would be, how happy his sisters would be, how happy he was, how beautiful Mughain was. Actually, Brendan had done most of the talking.

Mughain looked at the tide again. She was leaning against Brendan with her head against his shoulder, and she never wanted to be anywhere else. She glanced up at the sun. It was mid-afternoon; they had been sitting on the beach, kissing and talking and planning, for hours.

Gwyneth. Mughain looked around. Gwyneth was curled up asleep like a mermaid in the sand, next to a small sand farmhouse she had apparently built. It had a thatched straw roof and a little fence around it made of sticks. The tide was creeping toward it. It looked very fragile.

Reluctantly, Mughain moved away from Brendan and looked up at him. He smiled down at her. She had never seen anyone so beautiful. He kissed her again. "I need to go check

43

on Gwyneth," she said.

Brendan helped her up (for some reason, her legs felt shaky) and they padded through the sand to Gwyneth. She was not asleep; her eyes were open and she was staring at the little sand farmhouse. "Gwyneth?" Mughain said.

Gwyneth slowly stood up and brushed the sand from her dress. She leaned over and took some of the straw from the roof of the little house, and then trailed behind Brendan and Mughain as they started back toward the hall.

"Will you be bringing Gwyneth?" asked Brendan.

Mughain nodded. "She's mine, Father gave her to me." She glanced back at Gwyneth. The golden-haired girl was still following, but kept looking back at the little sand house.

"My mother and sisters – everyone – will be nice to her," said Brendan.

Mughain looked up at him. She thought she would get lost in his eyes and never find her way out. "Tonight," he said. "I'll ask your father tonight."

They walked back to the hall together. The sand was warm, and the gulls still circled and cried. Gwyneth looked back over her shoulder.

The king's men were still milling around the harbor. They had partially dismantled the wreck of Congal's ship and stacked the timbers on the beach. Some of the timbers could be reused, but some were broken and would have to be cut up for firewood.

The king was stomping around and shouting orders. Being a king, he could do no manual labor himself. It would lessen his honor. But a king was not born a king, and Tiernan knew all about ships and shipbuilding. If he occasionally picked up a hammer to work on his own ships, his men pretended not to notice.

"Too bad it couldn't be saved," said Brendan.

Some of the other boats had been damaged too. Some of the men had turned one over on the sand to patch a hole in its side. It had been a bad storm.

Neither the king, his sons, nor his men seemed to notice

Mughain and Brendan standing by the harbor. Brendan snorted and turned away. "They could ask me to help, you know," he said. "I've worked on lots of boats."

"Where's Gwyneth?" said Mughain.

Gwyneth was standing on the beach, staring back in the direction they had come. Mughain gently turned her around and steered her back up the rocky path to the hall.

In the courtyard, pork was roasting on spits over open fires. Mughain was glad. Roast pork was her father's favorite food. He needed to be in a good mood tonight.

Brendan looked down at Mughain and smiled. Her heart beat faster. "If I stay around you, I'm going to kiss you," he said quietly.

"That wouldn't be a good idea."

"True." Brendan sighed regretfully and headed off toward the stables.

Mughain took Gwyneth into the hall. It was not quite time for the daymeal, and she wanted to be alone for a little while to think. Gwyneth headed automatically for Mughain's room, and Mughain followed her, past the maids who were weaving the queen's new wall hangings (clickety-clack) and past the queen herself and her women, who were sitting on the dais and talking quietly together.

In her room, Mughain shook the sand out of her dress, flopped on the bed, and smiled at the thatched ceiling. She was going to marry Brendan. She was going to marry Brendan, and live close to the sea. It seemed too good to be true.

It occurred to her that she had not told Gwyneth. Gwyneth had been with them all afternoon, yet had discreetly not been paying any attention to them while she built her little sand farmhouse.

"Gwyneth," Mughain said and turned her head. Gwyneth was curled up on her pallet, facing the wall. "Brendan is going to ask Father for me."

Gwyneth didn't move. Mughain had a sudden, terrible thought. She and Brendan and Gwyneth had spent a lot of time together the last few days. Gwyneth had been born free, she was used to making her own choices. What if Gwyneth – what if she had feelings for Brendan?

A wave of anger threatened to engulf Mughain, like the stormwave that had sent Congal's half-built ship crashing to its doom. Gwyneth was very pretty. Brendan had asked if she was bringing Gwyneth with her. Brendan was *hers*, and he wasn't going to have any other wives or any concubines among his servants. "Gwyneth," she said sharply. Gwyneth cringed.

Instantly, the wave of anger was overwhelmed by a much larger wave of remorse. She was acting like her mother. How could she speak so to Gwyneth? Gwyneth who had suffered so much that Mughain could hardly imagine? "Gwyneth," she said much more gently, "Gwyneth, do you – I mean, do you *mind* about me and Brendan?"

Gwyneth turned her head and gave Mughain a very strange look. Her left eyebrow was up and her right eyebrow was down.

Mughain was relieved. Gwyneth apparently didn't care anything about Brendan. But something was wrong with her.

"Are you sick?"

Gwyneth just lay there.

It hit Mughain like a thunderbolt. "I'm not going to leave you here, Gwyneth! You're mine, I'll take you with me, of course."

Some of the tension went out of Gwyneth's shoulders, but she still lay facing the wall.

Mughain sat up on her bed and looked at her handmaiden. Gwyneth had been acting strangely all day – even for Gwyneth. No, it hadn't been all day. She had been all right when they walked down to the beach.

The beach reminded her of Brendan, but she pushed him out of her mind. Something had gone wrong with Gwyneth. Mughain unbraided her hair and combed it out while she thought. They had gone to the harbor to see the ships and walked along the beach, and then she had taken her shoes off and gone wading and Brendan had kissed her . . .

Gwyneth. She had built a little house in the sand and watched the tide come closer while Mughain and Brendan had talked and kissed . . .

Suddenly the details of the house came back to Mughain. A little, fragile sand farmhouse with a thatched seagrass roof and a stick fence, waiting for the tide to come and sweep it all away.

It had been her house – Gwyneth's house – Gwyneth's and her family's – and it was gone.

Mughain crept across the room and sat next to Gwyneth. The golden-haired girl was crying silently, hopelessly into her pallet.

There was nothing Mughain could do. In her own happiness she had not noticed what she normally would have – the fact that Gwyneth had aimlessly built a message in the sand. She curled up on the floor next to her handmaiden. At least she would not cry alone.

CHAPTER VI
IN HALL

The rumble of benches from the hall woke Mughain. She had fallen asleep on the floor next to Gwyneth's pallet, and the men were setting the benches and tables for the daymeal.

Gwyneth was asleep too. Mughain got up and changed into her green dress with gold embroidery. Her blue one still felt full of sand. Then she braided her hair carefully, in two braids like her mother's, and tied the ends with gold wire. It was a special night.

Gwyneth stirred and sat up. Mughain helped her wash her face and comb her hair, and they went together through the curtains and into the hall.

A few men were still putting benches in place, but the low tables were mostly full. The cooks were bringing in huge platters of steaming pork. It smelled good, but Mughain didn't think she could eat anything. A thousand butterflies were cavorting in her stomach. She found Brendan in the smoky torchlight, sitting about halfway down one of the lower tables. The butterflies multiplied.

She sat down next to her mother and Gwyneth took her place behind her chair. Her mother turned to look at her, said nothing, and turned her gaze back to the hall.

The king stomped in and took his seat. The hall grew quiet.

"Friends, welcome to my hall and to my table. By the grace of God, the damage from the storm is not so great as it could have been."

On the other side of the king, Congal snorted.

"Don't worry, boy, we'll build you a new ship." The king shook his head. "It's not the ship that's important, anyway." His eyes took on a faraway look, gazing out through the walls to the troubled sea his ancestors had sailed for generations. "As long as you've got the sea and the knowledge – you can always build a new ship."

The hall waited expectantly.

"But here I am talking!" said the king. "I'm as bad as the priest. Eat and drink! Shut the doors and shut out the night! We'll have no more talk of storms till morning." And the king helped himself to a leg of pork.

Everyone had worked hard all day, and everyone was hungry and thirsty. Laughter went around with the ale. Mughain tried to eat, but the food had no taste and had to fight with the butterflies. So she watched Brendan instead. He caught her eye and winked.

That did not help the butterflies.

It had to be the longest meal that was ever eaten. The king was in a better mood than Mughain had feared. He kept assuring Congal that they would build him an even better ship.

"I liked that one," Congal muttered sullenly.

"Well, the sea didn't," the king finally snapped, "she said she wouldn't have her, so we'll build her a new one." And he took a long drink to wash down all those confusing thoughts. Congal subsided. It was hard to argue with the sea.

Finally, the king had eaten enough and the meal was over. He rose and smiled on the hall, at the two long tables that reached back into the shadows by the door. "Friends, the daymeal is over."

Everyone cheered.

"Have we any business this evening? I am here, I will listen."

Brendan stood up, walked around the table and up to stand before the king. His blue tunic was carefully brushed; his hair glistened in the torchlight; one pointed ear showed slightly. Mughain could hardly breathe.

Brendan lifted his chin. "My lord king," he said, loudly and clearly. "I am Brendan, son of Conall son of Comhgall, prince of Dal Riata."

Everyone leaned forward slightly. Clearly, this was important business.

"Brendan son of Conall, son of Comhgall, you are welcome to my hall," said the king no less formally.

49

If it was possible, Brendan stood up even straighter. "I am a prince, of a good house," he repeated. "I am of age with sufficient fortune. I ask for your daughter Mughain."

The hall drew its breath and looked at the king.

"No," the king said.

The hall drew breath again, and looked at Brendan. He flushed. Before he could say anything, Mughain stood up. *"Why?"*

"Sit down, Mughain," said the king.

"No!" Mughain felt like she was going to cry, and scream, and hit someone, all at the same time.

"Lord king," said Brendan, "I make an honorable request, in hall. Why am I refused?" He was obviously trying very hard to keep his temper. "I know I am here as a hostage —"

The king made a dismissive gesture. "That has nothing to do with it. You've behaved with honor."

Brendan was quivering like a nervous horse. "Then why am I refused?"

"I have my reasons," said the king.

"What reasons?" demanded Mughain. The hall looked at her. Her mother looked at her, then looked away.

The king was starting to look irritated. "Maybe I have plans to marry you to someone else," he said. "Maybe I'll marry you to the priest."

That was ridiculous. "You're marrying Ita to the priest!" yelled Mughain.

"I'll marry *both* of you to the priest!" roared the king.

"My lord, I demand an answer!" said Brendan.

This was going too far; one could ask favors of a king, one could speak one's mind to a king, but one did not demand of a king. The hall went utterly silent. Brendan stood with his feet apart and his head thrown back. I'm going to lose him, thought Mughain. He will leave this hall and I will never see him again.

The king looked at Brendan, and he did not look very angry. "It's because of your grandmother," he said simply.

Brendan's hand flinched toward the hilt of his sword. "My

grandmother," he said slowly, "was a good Christian woman."

"So she was," said the king. "I mean no dishonor, and I've never heard a word spoken against her character or actions. But you know what I mean, boy."

"Say it," said Brendan through clenched teeth.

The king looked exasperated. "She was an elf."

Mughain looked at Brendan. She looked at his pointed ears, his skin that seemed to soften and reflect the light differently than other mortals. She wondered why she hadn't realized sooner.

Brendan was standing as though frozen, staring at the king. "Everyone knows, lad," said the king. "She couldn't help being what she was. But I don't want half-human grandsons."

That's all I am to my father, Mughain thought. I'm not a son, but I could be a provider of grandsons.

"The answer," said the king, "is no."

Brendan stared at him.

"Take word to your father," said the king. "I have considered the matter of the dispute between us, and I seem to remember that the cows in question are his. This information escaped my memory before, as I was busy with other matters. A hostage is no longer necessary. Go tomorrow morning and tell him."

The king sat down, looking displeased. Brendan turned stiffly and walked back to his chair. Only Mughain remained standing.

The torches flickered and the fires crackled. Then the bard plucked a few notes on his harp. Mughain felt a gentle tug on the back of her dress and turned around. It was Gwyneth, her eyes full of distress, urging her to sit down. Her legs seemed to have gone numb, but she awkwardly lowered herself into her chair.

The queen said something to the king that Mughain could not hear. "I can't let him stay now," the king muttered back. "Not after I've refused him. He'll be sulking around feeling dishonored. Let him go home and find some other pretty girl."

Mughain's hands clenched in her lap. The queen turned

and looked at Mughain. She looked at her for a long time.

*   *   *

It was impossible to talk to Brendan that night. During the flurry of putting tables and benches away and readying the hall for the night, a cordon of the king's men somehow stayed between them. It was not obvious; they did not stand in a line and guard, but they might as well have. Brendan stood and stared at Mughain, frustration in his eyes, until he turned on his heel and strode out into the courtyard.

Mughain's mother kept watching her. It was impossible to tell what she was thinking.

Mughain lingered in the hall, but Brendan did not come back. Finally she allowed a worried Gwyneth to lead her to her room.   She sat dully while Gwyneth removed the ceremonial gold wire ties from her braids and combed out her hair. Gwyneth's eyes were distressed and her forehead was furrowed. She tugged her mistress's green dress off, and when she did not lie down, gently pushed her over onto her pillow.

Mughain did not care if she were awake or asleep, alive or dead. Brendan. Perhaps he had already left, without saying goodbye. Perhaps he was riding through the forest in the dark, scowling and letting Fergus run. Perhaps he would forget her, and find some other pretty girl as the king had said.

Mughain knew that she would never forget, and that she would linger here alone until the end of days.

She slept a little, but felt more tired when she woke in the gray dawn than when she lay down. Brendan. She pulled on her gray and silver dress and allowed Gwyneth to comb and braid her hair, in two braids tied together at the back. Then she went out into the hall.

The men were stirring, yawning and picking up the pallets. Brendan stood outside the door in the soft rain.

She went to him. No one seemed to be standing guard. "You're leaving?"

Brendan looked older than he had last night. His face was set and determined. He wore his sword and cloak, and Fergus stood saddled and stomping, ready to go.

52

"I made you this," said Brendan. He handed her the wood carving she had seen him working on the day of the storm – the carving she had thought was a fish.

It wasn't a fish – it was a mermaid. Her face looked a little like Mughain's and her long hair swept down and concealed the fact that she wore nothing else. Her fish's tail curled up delicately beside her.

"It's beautiful," said Mughain. At least she would have something to remember him by.

"You're beautiful," said Brendan. His eyes were fixed on her, greenish-brown stones; he did not smile; his jaw was set.

"I will have you, if you want me," he said quietly. "I will bring my brothers and cousins, and we will take you home with us."

Mughain took a step back. Ritual kidnapping. Not common, now, but not unheard-of. It would allow her to be with Brendan, to marry Brendan, but it would be a battle between Brendan and his men and the king and his, and people would probably die. Maybe Brendan. It would also put Dal nAraide and Dal Riata at war, maybe for generations. She did not want it to be that way.

"Is there any other way?" Brendan asked softly. It was her own thought.

"I want to be your wife," she said. His jaw relaxed slightly. "But I do not want to destroy two kingdoms. I want to come to you freely, honorably. Not as a captive."

He looked at her. Mughain tried to memorize his face, his ears, his straight nose and hazel eyes, his hair that blew softly in the wind from the sea, his lips – his eyebrows that were steadily drawing together.

"Wait a month," she said. "I'll try to talk to my father. A month. If I do not send a messenger, or come to Dunseverick within that time – then come for me."

Brendan smiled. It was a grim smile, that saw the death of his kinsmen if they entered Lisnalinchy with force, but at least he had two eyebrows again.

"I cannot kiss you," he said, his voice full of longing. Too many people were in the courtyard, not exactly watching them.

"I love you," said Mughain. He picked up her hand and pressed it to his cheek. His eyes burned into hers.

"One month," they whispered at the same time, and grinned. He turned away, vaulted into Fergus' saddle, and galloped out of the gate.

Mughain did not think she would ever see him again.

The moon was still visible in the early morning sky, a faint, perfect half-circle. She would wax full, wane to nothing, and begin to wax again, and then it would be decided.

Mughain realized she was standing by herself in the middle of the courtyard, staring at the early morning moon. This was not accomplishing anything. It started to rain softly again as she turned to go inside.

CHAPTER VII
FASTING THE KING

"Anyone may approach the king."

Mughain looked up, surprised to hear the queen's voice. It was the morning after Brendan's departure, and the sky dripped gray rain. Mughain sat on a bench in the hall, staring at the wall, with Gwyneth curled up at her feet.

"What do you mean?" said Mughain. She had approached the king with her opinions the night before Brendan left, and it hadn't done much good.

The queen regarded her. "Remember Breasal son of Corval?" she said, and glided off.

"Breasal?" said Mughain blankly. Gwyneth looked at her. Breasal was an old man who had – *fasted the king*.

"I could fast him," said Mughain.

Gwyneth looked at her.

Mughain had never heard of a woman fasting a king, but she supposed it could be done. After all, her mother had suggested it. Sort of. The proper thing to do, of course, would be to send a male kinsman – but the thought of sending one of her brothers was almost laughable. They were just copies of her father, without his force and vitality. They would never help her against him.

So at dusk, just before the daymeal, Mughain wrapped herself in her warm white wool cloak, and exited the gates of Lisnalinchy. Then she turned to face them, and said clearly, "One has come to fast the king."

The king's men looked at her. "What do you mean, Mughain?" one of them said. His name was Terval, and he was only a few years older then herself.

Mughain stomped her foot. "I mean, I'm going to fast Father, so go tell him!"

Terval shook his head, but he and the other men closed the gates, leaving Mughain outside and very much alone. She had not brought Gwyneth. Somehow, she felt that this was something she should do alone. It had stopped raining during the day, but the sky was still gray and no color showed from the sunset, only deepening darkness.

Mughain heard Terval's voice from inside the hall. "Mughain, daughter of Tiernan, comes to fast the king," he announced.

There was a dead silence. Before, Mughain had heard a muted sound of talking and bustling about before eating; now there was nothing. Nothing until the king swore loudly, and there was a noise that sounded rather like a wooden platter slammed onto the table.

The gate opened and Terval stuck his head out. "The king is being fasted," he said formally, and shut the gate.

Smells of food drifted out through the gate, roast beef and leeks and fresh-baked bread. Mughain's stomach grumbled. She had expected this. The king did not have to hear her petition right away – but he could not eat until he did. Of course, neither could she. So she wrapped her cloak more tightly around her and turned to face the night.

It was getting dark – very dark. Mughain had never been outside her father's walls at night before. She could barely make out trees that were not far away. There was no moon. The world was being sucked into a silent gray void.

Perhaps she could look out to sea – or towards it – and that would help. She walked to the edge of the wall and around the corner, and froze.

She could not see the sea. Instead, she saw a great wave of fog rolling up the shore, engulfing everything in its path. It was taller than she was, and glowed with a faint white light. It swallowed Mughain's rock chair and flowed relentlessly toward the hall.

Mughain scurried around the wall and back to the gates. She dropped in front of them and covered her head with her cloak. The fog was coming for her. It would flow around the sides of the hall and envelop her and she would never be seen or heard from again. All the stories she had half-heard in whispers all her life came back to her – rumors of an angry sea, stories of spirits in the night, of holes in the forest floor to trap the unwary, of tiny lights set to mislead travelers and strange paths twisting to snare unwary virgins. She *felt* the fog coming nearer, felt its malevolence and its hatred for her and her kind. She cowered under her cloak and prayed desperately to the God of St. Patrick.

And there before her father's gates, she knew suddenly that the God of St. Patrick had heard, and that He was greater and more powerful than the spirits of the night and the fog. She could almost hear their howl of frustration as they ebbed away.

The gates opened, and Terval stuck his head out. He looked with some concern at Mughain, huddled in her cloak at his feet. "The king will hear the petitioner," he said.

Mughain stood up unsteadily and shook out her cloak. She would never be afraid of the dark again. Fog blanketed the ground, but it was an ordinary gray fog without that eerie and malevolent white light. She passed into the courtyard and Terval shut the gate behind her. "Foggy," he said.

Mughain walked through the courtyard and into the hall. Every eye was upon her. No one was eating. She walked the length of the hall, past the long benches and the firepits and the whispers, to the head table, where her father sat furious in his place. The queen sat next to him under her canopy; Mughain's brothers looked at her with varying levels of blankness, annoyance, and speculation; Gwyneth stood behind Mughain's chair looking worried.

"Speak," the king snarled, "and you will be heard."

Mughain took a deep breath. "Let me marry Brendan," she said. "Please."

"No," said the king. He picked up a chunk of roast beef and tore off an unnecessarily large bite.

Mughain walked around the table, through the leather curtain, and into her room as a buzz of talk broke out in the hall. Gwyneth followed her.

*   *   *

It was impossible to plan. She could not leave the hall, even to go sit on her rock chair to look at the sea, without the

57

king's men hovering around, deliberately and ostentatiously not watching her. A week went by, then another, then another. Gwyneth trailed around after her, looking concerned. The moon had waxed to the full, remorselessly bright over the hall, and waned slowly, inexorably, to the thinnest of silver crescents, ready for her disappearance and rebirth.

But one morning the king was in a rage. It was something about cows. Mughain wasn't really paying attention – some cows weren't where they were supposed to be. But after breaking their fast, the men started loading the king's ship with food and arrows and spare clothing.

Mughain stood at the wall and watched some of the men carrying a roasted side of beef down to the harbor. The sea was greenish gray today, sending little gusts of wind up over the rocks to tug at her green dress. Surely her father wasn't going to just leave, and go pick a fight over some cows. Certainly he had done it before. But now? Did he think she had forgotten Brendan already? Or did she just not matter enough?

The king was coming up the beach with his eldest son. His face was eager. "With these winds, we'll reach the cliffs in two days." They circled the wall and passed Mughain. They did not even seem to see her.

The daymeal that evening was tense and excited. The tables buzzed with masculine talk – sails, provisions, weapons, winds. The queen sat icy and disapproving under her canopy. There was no music and no singing.

When the king had eaten enough, he stood up and said, "We sail at dawn!"

There were loud cheers.

When they had lessened, the king continued, "I leave Lisnalinchy in the hands of my queen until my return."

There was more cheering, polite and not as loud. The king turned to Queen Nessa and said something in her ear. Without expression, she turned her head to her left to look at Mughain.

Mughain was sure men would be left behind to watch her.

The morning was clear and cold with a silver sea. Gwyneth helped Mughain put on her gray dress and they went down to the harbor with the rest of the household to see the king's departure.

The harbor was busy with men, loading last-minute items, checking the ship and the sail. The priest stood uncomfortably to one side. He refused to bless such a journey, but he did offer a prayer for the king's safe return.

Finally the ship was pushed out into the harbor, and the oars lowered. They pulled in rhythm and one of the men began a song:

> "Sail away at dawn
> To find my true love
> Sail away at dawn
> While the day is young
>
> Sail away at dawn
> When the world is waking
> Sail away at dawn
> When the sky is gold
>
> Sail away at dawn
> While the breeze is freshening
> Sail away at dawn
> As the morning comes . . ."

The king stood at the prow of the boat, gazing ahead out to sea. At the harbor mouth, the men raised the big square sail and pulled in the oars. The ship turned slightly as the sail filled, tipped precariously but righted itself and ran under the wind, around the harbor mouth and out of sight, a fragile toy boat on the immensity of the sea. They could still hear the men singing.

> "Sail away at dawn
> While the night is dying . . ."

Mughain walked back up the rocky slope to the hall. Those with work outside scattered to their tasks – the grooms to the stables, the servants who were repairing the latest damage to the wall by the ever-present sea winds. She and Gwyneth followed the queen and her women into the hall, and without any sort of plan, went to Mughain's room.

Mughain lay down on her bed and Gwyneth perched on her pallet and looked at her.

The leather curtain was pushed aside and the queen entered the room.

Mughain sat up. "Mother!" she said. The queen never came to see her.

"Do you love him?" said the queen.

Mughain looked at her blankly.

"This Brendan, do you love him?"

"Yes," Mughain said slowly.

The queen pondered. As usual, very little expression crossed her face, but she pondered.

"The king," she said finally, "has great respect for the church." Her lips twisted slightly.

Mughain stared at her. She looked at Gwyneth for enlightenment, but she looked just as puzzled as Mughain felt.

"If you and Brendan were married by a priest," said the queen, "the king would accept it as binding. The king will be away for several days."

She gave Mughain a look that was expressionless yet somehow meaningful, and glided from the room.

Mughain and Gwyneth stared at each other. "Did she just tell me I could leave?" Mughain said slowly.

Gwyneth's forget-me-not blue eyes were wide. Mughain thought it over. The queen was in charge; the queen had said she could go marry Brendan. If a Christian priest married her to Brendan before her father found out, he might not be happy, but probably wouldn't come after her with his men. At least that was what the queen had seemed to be saying.

"Let's start packing," said Mughain. She had never felt quite so close to her mother before – perhaps because she had never before understood that her mother was capable of only one kind of love.

CHAPTER VIII
THE ROAD TO DAL RIATA

At first, they tried to be discreet in their preparations. Mughain sorted out the things she wanted to take with her. She was wearing her gray dress; she lay her blue and green dresses out on her bed, along with her white wool cloak, some shifts, needle and thread, a few other things she might need, the mermaid Brendan had made her, and wrapped them in a gray wool blanket. The blanket had been woven by her mother herself.

She had sent Gwyneth to get food. She came back staggering under a large sack full of bread, cheese, dried beef, and dried apples.

Mughain looked at what they planned to take with them. She realized with a pang that she would not see this year's apples ripen in the orchard, or join with everyone to pick them, all distinctions gone, skirts tied up to climb to the highest branches, ducking apples that Rory threw at her, watching her father pour the first cider under the trees as an offering to the orchard while the priest looked on disapprovingly . . .

She tore her mind back to the present, back to the pile of things they were sneaking away with. "They're never going to believe we're going on a picnic."

So they started by taking a few small bundles at a time to the stables, but no one seemed to notice. Indeed, everyone seemed to be purposefully looking away from them and not noticing them at all. So they grew bolder and took Mughain's big bundle and some extra blankets all together. Still, no one seemed to notice, most likely on her mother's orders.

When almost everything was ready, the queen came to Mughain's room with some brown cloth over her arm. Mughain looked up, afraid the queen had changed her mind, but she had not. "You have three good gowns, but nothing suitable for — rougher wear," said her mother. "You may have this one." She gave her the brown cloth, and turned and left.

Mughain unfolded the dress. It was not old. It was exactly her size, well made but of rougher and sturdier wool than she usually wore. A tree with interweaving branches was embroidered in green around the neck – her mother's work. She must have been working on it for some time. She blinked back tears, but put the brown dress on and folded the gray one to go with the others. She and Gwyneth were now dressed much the same.

After that, Mughain threw all caution to the winds. She had a groom saddle two horses, a brown one and the white one Gwyneth liked, and tie on their saddlebags and bundles. Then she went and sat on her rock chair and looked out to sea. She was leaving; she would never sit here again, never again trace with a finger the faint markings on the rock that looked like they might once have been carvings. She would never again sit in the hall at daymeal next to her mother, and hear the king give hearty judgments and listen to the music of the bard's harp and sing with the others.

The sea sparkled below her, blue-green-gray. It was time to be going; it was almost noon and they had far to go. But she sat in her rock chair for some time later, until she stood, swung her red cloak around her shoulders, and went back into the courtyard for the last time.

Her mother was there waiting. Gwyneth, in her brown dress and too-short blue cloak, hovered around anxiously. "A fine day for an outing, my daughter," said the queen. She fastened Mughain's cloak around her neck and did something very rare – bent down and kissed her forehead.

"A fine day, mother," said Mughain with a lump in her throat.

"One should always be careful – even on a picnic," observed the queen. She glanced at the sack of food on Gwyneth's horse. "It is to be hoped that you will have the best and happiest of – picnics."

"I will try. Thank you, mother," said Mughain. It was all she could say. She and Gwyneth mounted their horses. Her mother walked her to the gate, and stood with the rest of the household as Mughain rode through. No one spoke.

They took the road Brendan had taken, away from the hall and toward the woods, which soon enveloped them and shut out all sound from the outside world. Mughain took a deep breath. She could see the road narrow and vanish into the trees at the edge of her sight. But Brendan was at the end of that road. She kept going.

They rode side by side, Mughain nervously keeping as close to the center of the road as she could without pushing Gwyneth off entirely. The branches seemed to be reaching out towards her, whispering. The sky was covered by them. They should have left earlier. But her heart still reached back crying for the sea.

They rode for several hours, stopped and had a bite to eat, and rode on. The trees were growing thicker and older, and less light came through them. Soon they would have to stop for the night.

Gwyneth veered off the road and dismounted next to a particularly large tree. Mughain followed her. It was ancient, hollow, with decaying bark and strange knots that looked like faces in the dusk. Its roots spread out around it like writhing skirts. Mughain peered inside reluctantly, thinking of all the things that could be inside – bears, weasels, fairies – but it seemed empty, and they needed shelter. It was the dark of the moon. They tied the horses to the tree's roots to let them graze, unloaded and unsaddled them, ate, and curled up together in the tree.

Mughain watched the darkness fall. She was afraid to go to sleep. What if there were fairies in the tree after all? It was said that they watched for unwary travelers. It was very dangerous to go to sleep in a fairy tree. You could wake up in another world and never be able to get back.

"Do you know anything about fairies?" she said.

Gwyneth opened her eyes and looked at her.

"Well, there *could* be fairies," Mughain muttered.

Gwyneth closed her eyes and settled herself to sleep.

Fairies or no fairies, Mughain woke up with green sunlight filtering down through the leaves and into the tree. She and Gwyneth crawled out, rather dirty, shook themselves out, greeted the horses, and sat down on the ground to eat.

Mughain was surprisingly hungry. At least the fairies had not taken her appetite. Between bites of bread and cheese and dried beef, she looked around her. The forest was surprisingly cheerful. The light was green but bright; the millions of leaves made tiny, cheerful rustling noises all around them. The tree they had slept in still looked a little strange, but sleepy and old. A small furry animal of a kind Mughain had never seen before dashed across the path. Gwyneth smiled.

Mughain was clumsy about saddling her horse, but Gwyneth helped her. Gwyneth seemed to be friends with her white mare, petting its nose and sides. The horse seemed to understand her perfectly. Mughain eyed her own horse. It was a perfectly good horse, but she would much rather have a boat.

They went on into the trees, leaving the fairy tree behind. Midmorning the path was crossed by a clear, bubbling brook. They drank and refilled their waterskins, splashed across and went on. The brook had once been a boundary line. Some very old stones, covered with moss, lay broken at its side. But Mughain knew they were still in her father's kingdom.

The forest grew quieter as they progressed. It was not a sinister silence; simply a *silent* silence, a reflecting, growing stillness. Mughain, and of course Gwyneth, did not talk either. When the green light was coming from straight overhead, they stopped and ate bread and cheese and apples; then they went on. All that long, golden afternoon they rode through the living arch of the forest. They saw two more of the small brown animals.

At dusk Mughain looked hopefully for another hollow tree, but none appeared. They had to settle for a flat spot next to a tree. But there they found –

"Mushrooms!" squealed Mughain.

Gwyneth looked at them doubtfully.

"It's all right, they're not poisonous," said Mughain.

Gwyneth's expression did not change.

"I know how to tell the difference," said Mughain, slightly offended. "Brona taught me. Do you know how to make a fire?"

Gwyneth's face cleared and she started gathering dry sticks. Nonetheless, Mughain looked very carefully at each mushroom. One of her half-brothers, the son of a maidservant, had died screaming from eating bad mushrooms. She did not intend for the same thing to happen to herself and Gwyneth.

She washed the mushrooms carefully and put them in a pot over the fire with some dried beef and a little water. By the time they were done the forest was completely dark, and they ate by firelight.

It was amazingly cheering to have a hot meal. The mushrooms were tender and wild-tasting. They ate every scrap out of the pot and then sat rolled up in their cloaks by the tiny fire.

It was a three-day journey they were making. They were halfway there. Mughain could not believe it was so easy.

But the next day was a very different kind of day. They woke with rain dripping on their faces from the trees overhead. They ate some more mushrooms (raw this time, with cheese, dried apples, and bread) and reloaded the horses. The horses were not pleased.

The morning grew darker and wetter and colder. The horses plodded along, and Gwyneth was shivering with her inadequate cloak wrapped tight around her. Mughain supposed she was shivering herself. They had to find shelter. They would lose half a day, but they could not go on.

She kept an eye out for a hollow tree, but did not find one. She put on her thick white cloak and gave her red one to Gwyneth, but her fingers were almost too cold to hold the reins. They dismounted and walked beside the horses to stay warm. She supposed they could make some sort of tent out of a blanket, but it seemed better to keep moving than to huddle miserably on the ground.

Then an old woman appeared suddenly in the murk of the

path before them.

She was a very strange old woman. Her brown dress and cloak were old and hung on her loosely and her gray hair stuck out in all directions, but a great light was in her eyes, shining through the dark and the rain.

"God and Mary be with you, my daughters," she said.

"God and Mary and Patrick be with you, my mother," replied Mughain automatically.

"It's no time to be out," said the woman. "Come into my house."

As though in a dream, they led their horses after her to a little house almost hidden by the trees. A holy woman. Some women lived alone, far from others, serving God.

"Come into the house," said the woman, "and bring our cousins. It's not fit out for them either, and I have no stable."

After a moment's hesitation, Mughain and Gwyneth unsaddled their horses and led them into the house after the strange old woman, under the St. Brigid's cross, woven of rushes, that hung over the door. The house was very small, and there was already a goat in one corner. But it was warm and dry. Aside from the goat, the one room contained a bed, two chairs, and a small firepit, where a pot was bubbling and sending out the most wonderful smells. Mughain's mouth watered, and she saw Gwyneth swallow.

"Take off your cloaks, children," said the old woman. "I am Mona. Welcome to my house."

"A blessing on the house," said Mughain, again automatically. They put the horses with the goat, who was eating hay, and took off their cloaks. Mona spread them next to the fire to dry. Mughain noticed that the bed was occupied by two of the little brown creatures they had seen in the forest, and a mouse.

"Sit down, sit down," said Mona. "It's a long hard journey you'll be having, I don't doubt." She asked no questions, but puttered around getting the food ready, adding herbs to the pot, breaking up a loaf of oatbread that had been baking on the stones of the hearth. Mughain offered the last of their cheese, which Mona accepted with a smile.

Soon, but not soon enough, the meal was done. It was a rich vegetable stew (including mushrooms). They ate and ate. Mughain didn't want to eat too much of the old woman's food, as she obviously lived in holy poverty, but Mona kept refilling their bowls.

When they had eaten enough, and were warm and dry, Mughain looked around the room with more interest. The horses and goat were munching hay. Gwyneth sat quietly staring at the fire, its light flickering off her gold hair.

"That's a pretty girl you've got," said the old woman to Mughain. "Saxon, is she?"

Mughain nodded. Mona must have noticed that Gwyneth didn't speak, but she asked no questions about it. In the firelight, Mughain noticed a few bright gold threads in Mona's gray hair.

The fire crackled. "Her name is Gwyneth," said Mughain.

Mona frowned. "Gwyneth? That's not a Saxon name." She paused. "Cwynthyth?"

Gwyneth jumped slightly and looked at Mona.

"Cwynth," Mughain tried. "Cwynthy." It was very hard to say. The men who had captured Gwyneth must have heard her family calling her name . . . under circumstances that made Mughain shiver to think of . . . and pronounced it Gwyneth. "Cwynthyth," she said finally, twisting her tongue around the strange syllables. She looked at Gwyneth proudly.

Gwyneth looked at her. There was a strange, closed expression on her face. Mughain knew she did not want to hear her real name spoken by the voices of her captivity.

Gwyneth she would remain.

The fire crackled. "Poor weather for travelers," said the old woman, "but the sun will come out tomorrow."

They curled up in their cloaks to sleep on the floor by the fire. The horses and goat rustled in their corner, and the rain dripped outside. But sure enough, when they woke in the morning, the sun shone with its filtered green light through the open door of the cottage. Mona was not there, but two bowls of last night's stew sat by the cold fire. The old woman had not reappeared before Mughain and Gwyneth finished their breakfast.

They washed the bowls and put them back on the table. Then they mucked out the corner where the horses had stayed, Gwyneth laughing her rare laughter when Mughain wrinkled her nose at the smell. When they were done, Mughain looked around and bit her lip anxiously. It was time for them to be going, but they had not thanked their hostess, and she had no parting gift to leave her. She looked through her possessions. Her clothes would not fit Mona, and Brendan's mermaid she would not part with. Finally she left her iron needle on the table under a bowl, to keep it safe from the small animals that apparently shared Mona's house. Gwyneth nodded in approval. It was a good needle.

"A blessing on the house," said Mughain as they rode away from the little hut with St. Brigid's cross over the door.

The sun shone through the leaves all that morning. The afternoon was long and green. They stopped to eat and rest a few minutes, and as they were getting back on their horses, something crashed through the trees toward them.

Gwyneth screamed. She turned her horse and bolted off in the opposite direction, directly into the forest.

Mughain was only halfway into her saddle. Out of the corner of her eye she glimpsed a huge shape in the trees behind them, gray with glints of gold. Her horse reared, but she somehow managed to vault over, clutching it around the neck. It plunged into the forest after Gwyneth. Mughain kept her head down, but branches slapped her head and arms. She felt her dress catch on a branch and tear. And then suddenly she heard Gwyneth scream again, they were out in the blinding sunlight with the sweep of the sea blue and sparkling before them, and then suddenly there was nothing beneath the horse's hooves.

The fall took an improbably long time, with the horse kicking its legs under her. She caught a glimpse of black rocks and smiling blue sea, and hit the water in a hard, wet tangle of horse's legs and dress and salt sea.

She seemed to have hit her head. The horse was no longer there. She wondered which way was up. Light and dark were all mixed up in all directions, and she couldn't remember how to swim.

Then a strong arm grabbed her around the waist, pulled her to a powerful torso and she was being propelled through the water very fast. She thought she caught a glimpse of a large fish's tail, but now all the light was leaving her and everything was dark.

CHAPTER IX
THE WAY TO THE SEA

Dry and warm, and sand under her toes, and light everywhere. Mughain slowly opened her eyes and looked up into Gwyneth's anxious face. The world seemed to be tilting in a strange way. She turned her head, and saw a strange sight. The head and bare chest of a man, a very beautiful man, was rising up out of the sea. He had long silvery-green hair and a square rugged face, and wore a coronet of seashells and pearls. Mughain blinked, and he was gone.

After awhile she opened her eyes again. She was lying on the beach with her head on Gwyneth's lap. Gwyneth looked very concerned. Mughain tried to smile, but it made her head hurt.

Gwyneth's hair had come unbraided in the water and hung around her face half-dried in a wild halo of gold. And around her neck was a necklace Mughain had never seen before, a beautiful necklace made of perfectly polished seashells.

Mughain reached up and touched it. "Where did you get that?"

Gwyneth smiled slightly. It was a look that Mughain had never seen on her face before.

After awhile Mughain sat up and looked around. Her head didn't hurt too badly. They were on a narrow beach. Behind it was a sheer black cliff reaching up and up and up . . . Mughain shuddered. To the east the beach narrowed and disappeared altogether into the rocks. That must have been where they had fallen over.

Mughain looked around for the horses. Amazingly they were both there, slightly damp, eating some grass that grew sparsely by the cliff.

Mughain got up, assisted by Gwyneth, and limped over to the horses. They seemed all right, and still had their saddlebags. The food was spoiled, of course, soaked in seawater. The clothes and blankets and other things they laid out in the sun to dry.

To the west the beach widened and the cliff became less steep. Mughain hoped they would be able to find a place to climb back up to the forest and find the road. If they followed the coast, they would come to Dal Riata in time; but it was a longer journey, there was no prospect of food, and more black cliffs reaching down to the water might make the way impassible.

Mugain sat down and rubbed her head. "How were we rescued?" she asked.

Gwyneth smiled her small secret smile.

Mughain wondered. She also wondered about the large gray shape in the woods that had spooked Gwyneth and sent them careening over the cliff.

As if she knew what Mughain was thinking, Gwyneth hung her head. "It's all right, Gwyneth," said Mughain. "It's not your fault. We've come to no harm." She hoped that whatever it was did not threaten Mona. But few things, whether wild beast or wild man or spirit of the night, would harm a holy woman.

The blankets and cloaks and dresses were dry, but stiff with salt and covered with sand. They shook them out, reloaded the horses, and plodded down the beach. It was slow going in the sand. Soon they came to a stream flowing down to the sea that tasted only a little like salt. But after drinking, they were even hungrier.

Cliff on the left, sea on the right, on and on. Gwyneth kept gazing out to sea and smiling her odd little smile.

At last the cliff dropped back sharply to join the forest, and they were able to lead the horses up over the rocks. This part of the forest was old. Once away from the sea, the trees were huge and tough, far too big for Mughain and Gwyneth to touch hands if they had stood on either side and wrapped their arms around. The roots extended far out in all directions, leaving the earth and reentering it, making arches too small to go under but too big to go over – so they had to go around. But after going around a maze of roots several times, Mughain was not quite sure what direction they were going. The sun was blocked by leaves and branches thick and dark. She had heard that moss grew on the north side of trees, but these trees seemed to have moss all over them.

The darkness deepened into night. Mughain found a few mushrooms and they ate them in the last of the dim light. Then they curled up at the foot of a tree to sleep.

Sleep did not come to Mughain. Her head ached where she had hit it. She wondered very much about their escape from the sea. She remembered being rescued by a very fast swimmer. Surely Gwyneth could not swim so fast. And what about that face she had seen rising up out of the water? But that was only because she had hit her head.

But what about Gwyneth's necklace?

She must have gone to sleep, because she woke with a new worry. Even if they found the path today, it was still a day and a half to Dal Riata. She had not seen the moon for several nights, but that did not keep it from waxing steadily. Soon Brendan would set out after her. She must reach Dal Riata before he did.

She looked over at Gwyneth. She was awake, her hair gold in the dim forest, gazing off with that peculiar smile on her lips.

"Gwyneth," said Mughain, "do you know how to get back to the sea?"

Gwyneth looked at her and nodded.

"Let's go back then," said Mughain. "If we keep close to the coast – not under the cliffs, but close to them – we will find out way. Otherwise —"

Gwyneth nodded. Otherwise they could wander in circles under the trees forever.

Mughain was utterly lost. She did not know how Gwyneth found their way back to the sea, but she did. They led the horses back through the maze of roots and branches, through the thick carpet of old leaves that drifted up against the trunks and hid treacherous footing beneath. The forest, Mughain felt, wanted them out. It was not a sinister feeling – simply a feeling that they did not belong. They were out of time with the slow-growing trees, rushing about on their legs where it was appropriate only to be still.

Then the trees opened out and the soil grew sandy, and salt blew in on the breeze. Mughain was so exhausted with relief and hunger and worry that she slipped off her horse and went to sleep on the ground.

*   *   *

When she woke up, she smelled fish cooking. Gwyneth was hovering over a small fire a few feet away, roasting two fish on sticks.

"Where did you get those fish?"

Gwyneth smiled.

The fish were wonderful, but messy. They went down to the sea to wash their hands. Late afternoon light slanted from the sun over the water. A few sleepy-sounding gulls cried and circled overhead.

"Gwyneth," said Mughain hesitantly, "what if I get there and – Brendan doesn't want me?"

Gwyneth gave her a look of scorn.

"It's been almost a month since I've seen him," said Mughain. "What if he —" Mughain remembered what her father had said – that Brendan would find himself another pretty girl.

Gwyneth patted her hand comfortingly. She did not seem at all concerned. But Mughain was. She looked to the west, in the direction that they must travel. A rocky overhang jutted up, swallowing the beach. She had been right to try to go back and find the path, because they could not follow the coast. But since they could not find the path, they must creep as close to the coast as possible, in the thin trees between the forest and the rocks, and try not to lose their way, and try to get there before Brendan left, and hope that Brendan had not found another pretty girl.

Two days they did this, living on mushrooms and seaweed and fish, while the silver crescent of the moon swelled and grew brighter every night. Mughain never saw Gwyneth catch the fish. She was always cooking them with a smile when Mughain woke up in the morning.

Then, at the end of the second day, they hit a path coming out of the trees toward the shore. It was the beginning of the end of the road to Dal Riata.

They camped by the road that night, and Mughain kept hearing in her dreams the hoofbeats of a party of young men riding off to war.

When she woke there was no smell of fish cooking, and no Gwyneth.

Mughain jumped up and looked around her. "Gwyneth?"

Her brown horse was still tied to a tree, looking at her inquisitively, but Gwyneth's white one was gone.

Mughain ran down to the beach. On the sand in the shadow of the trees, neatly folded, was Gwyneth's brown dress. The blue embroidery Mughain had added was carefully displayed on top.

She picked up the dress and clasped it to her. Off in the dazzling distance of the sea she thought she saw three large fishtails flash – one silver, one gold, one white.

*   *   *

The last hours were long with hunger and grief. Mughain had put on her blue dress with the red embroidery, combed her hair carefully, and braided it in two braids tied with gold wires. She would not appear at the gate of Brendan's father's hall looking like a beggar. She rode out of the woods entirely, and the sea opened its arms to her, bluer and bluer to a lost and murky horizon. It was the same sea she had always known, that had called to her since she was a child and had led her here.

The road wound around a bluff, and suddenly there before her, on a promontory reaching out to sea, was Dal Riata. It was much like her father's house, a wooden wall enclosing the roofs of a hall and other buildings, but all encircled and enclosed by the sea, except for a narrow spit of land covered by the gate.

These gates were open, and a group of young men were

riding forth. The first one was Brendan on Fergus, the sun glinting on his hair, his eyebrows pulled together. But when he saw Mughain, his expression changed altogether.

"Mughain!" he yelled.

Several things happened in the next few seconds. Brendan galloped towards her, leaped off his horse, lifted Mughain off hers, and the world turned upside down because he kissed her, all very fast.

"We were just coming for you," he said.

He was real; his arms were solidly around her, and apparently he had not found another pretty girl. Over his shoulder she could see his kinsman, and she had to smile. Brendan and his brothers and cousins all looked ridiculously alike. Some of their hair was slightly lighter brown, some darker; some were a little older or a little younger, but all had the same heavy eyebrows and the same slightly pointed ears. Some of those eyebrows were drawing together now in frowns. They had been cheated of their dangerous and uncertain adventure.

But Brendan's face shone like the sea as he took her hand. "Come on, let's go inside," he said. Then he looked around. "Where's Gwyneth?"

Mughain glanced out to sea. She could not feel so sad anymore. "Gwyneth," she said, "has been freed."

Brendan looked a little confused. But he asked no questions, took her horse's reins, and led Mughain through the gates of Dal Riata. Two young women ran out of the hall, one with red hair and one with brown hair and pointed ears, and looked smiling and inquisitive at Brendan and Mughain.

"Welcome home, princess," he said.

The waves crashed on the rocks. The seabirds circled and cried as the household came out to greet her.

About the author . . .

Jennifer Sparlin's short stories and poetry have appeared in *Beyond Centauri, Renaissance Magazine, Writers' Journal, Flint Hills Review, The Midwest Quarterly,* and *Crow Toes Quarterly.* Her travel writing and letter to the editor have been published in *The Wichita Eagle* and *The New York Times.* She has won several awards, including a Letter of Merit in the Society of Children's Book Writers and Illustrators Magazine Merit Awards. She holds a BFA in Theatre Arts and an MA in Communication and Theatre/Drama, and teaches at Butler Community College.

Much of the inspiration for *The Sea at Mughain* came from a memorable trip to Ireland, where Jennifer encountered fog, sheep, indecipherable street signs, and strange, ancient beauty.

Jennifer lives in Wichita, Kansas, with her husband and cats.